With the
compliments
of the
Canada Council

Avec les
hommages
du Conseil des
Arts du Canada

Rat Jelly

Rat Jelly

Michael Ondaatje

1943–

The Coach House Press Toronto

Contents

for Christopher and Janet and Gillian
for my Mother and in memory of my Father

Families

She said, 'What about Handy? Think I should send it to him?'
'He's supposed to call in a little while. I'll ask him.'
'He retired, didn't he?'
'Yes.'
She waited and then said, 'Say something, Parker. God to get you
to gossip it's like pulling teeth.'
'Handy retired.' Parker said.
'I *know* he retired! Tell me about it. Tell me why he retired, tell
me where he is, how he's doing. Talk to me, Parker, goddammit.'

Richard Stark, *The Sour Lemon Score*

War Machine

Think I dont like people   NO
like some dont like many
love wife kids dogs couple of friends
hate art which what all talk about
all the time is what they talk about
like monopoly volleyball cards ping pong
tennis late movies hitchcock sergio leone
movie scandal O I can tell you stories
30 jayne mansfield stories that
will give erections all around the room
they'll come at you like non-fiction whips
stories too bout vivien leigh princess margaret
frank sinatra the night he beat up mia farrow

Perhaps
wd like to live mute
all day long
not talk

just listen to the loathing

Gold and Black

At night the gold and black slashed bees come
pluck my head away. Vague thousands drift
leave brain naked stark as liver
each one carries atoms of flesh, they
walk my body in their fingers.
The mind stinks out.

In the black Kim is turning
a geiger counter to this pillow.
She cracks me open like a lightbulb.

Love, the real,
terrifies
the dreamer in his riot cell.

Letter to Ann Landers

Dear Ann Landers
            I get really
turned on by flies
crawling over my body
I keep telling my husband (of 14 years)
that this is normal
and that people all over the world
feel the same way but he says
he feels jealous especially
as I'm always tired
when he comes to bed

It *is* true Ann I *do* feel worn out
it is the flies (I mean it are the flies)
after an hour or two with them
I'm finished and
don't want anyone else touching me
My husband thinks putting
honey on my body is going too far

I love my husband Ann
would you please reply to this
so I could show him your answer
and make him feel
not so left out of things

Billboards

'Even his jokes were exceedingly drastic.'

My wife's problems with husbands, houses,
her children that I meet
at stations in Kingston, in Toronto, in London Ontario
— they come down the grey steps
bright as actors after their drugged four hour ride
of spilled orange juice and comics
(when will they produce a gun and shoot me
at Union Station by Gate 4?)
Reunions for Easter egg hunts
kite flying, Christmases.
They descend on my shoulders every holiday.
All this, I was about to say,
disturbs, invades my virgin past.

When she lay beginning
this anthology of kids
I moved — blind but senses
jutting faux pas, terrible humour,
shifted with a sea of persons,
breaking when necessary
into smaller self sufficient bits of mercury.
My mind a carefully empty diary
till I hit the barrier reef
that was my wife —
                                there
the right bright fish
among the coral.

With her came the locusts of history —
innuendoes she had missed
varied attempts at seduction (even rape)
dogs who had been bred
and killed by taxis or brain disease.
Numerous problems I was unequal to.
Here was I trying to live
with a neutrality so great
I'd have nothing to think of,
just to sense
and kill it in the mind.
Nowadays I somehow get the feeling
I'm in a complex situation,
one of several billboard posters
blending in the rain.

I am writing this with a pen my wife has used
to write a letter to her first husband.
On it is the smell of her hair.
She must have placed it down between sentences
and thought, and driven her fingers round her skull
gathered the slightest smell of her head
and brought it back to the pen.

Kim, at half an inch

Brain is numbed
is body touch
and smell, warped light

hooked so close
her left eye
is only a golden blur
her ear a vast
musical instrument of flesh

The moon spills off my shoulder
slides into her face

Somebody sent me a tape

Yellow flowers against the fridge
in front of it the
tape slides round
Gary Snyder is reading in Michigan
a year ago his
voice shakes my cigarette smoke
we are sliding round
and round yellow
flowers against the fridge
hot yellow
in Toronto Kim is giving
her sick mother flowers
here a milk jug an opened letter
cigarettes ashtray my
in front of me
other hand on the table

Notes for the legend of Salad Woman

Since my wife was born
she must have eaten
the equivalent of two-thirds
of the original garden of Eden.
Not the dripping lush fruit
or the meat in the ribs of animals
but the green salad gardens of that place.
The whole arena of green
would have been eradicated
as if the right filter had been removed
leaving only the skeleton of coarse brightness.

All green ends up eventually
churning in her left cheek.
Her mouth is a laundromat of spinning drowning herbs.
She is never in fields
but is sucking the pith out of grass.
I have noticed the very leaves from flower decorations
grow sparse in their week long performance in our house.
The garden is a dust bowl.

On our last day in Eden as we walked out
she nibbled the leaves at her breasts and crotch.
But there's none to touch
none to equal
the Chlorophyll Kiss

Postcard from Piccadilly Street

Dogs are the unheralded voyeurs of this world.
When we make love
the spaniel shudders
walks out of the room,
she's had her fill of children now

but the bassett — for whom
we've pretty soon got to find a love object
apart from furniture or visitors' legs —
jumps on the bed and watches.

It is a catching habit having a spectator
and appeals to the actor in both of us,
in spite of irate phone calls from the SPCA
who claim we are corrupting minors
(the dog being one and a half).

We have moved to elaborate audiences now.
At midnight we open the curtains
turn out the light
and imagine the tree outside
full of sparrows
with infra red eyes.

The Strange Case

My dog's assumed my alter ego.
Has taken over — walks the house
phallus hanging wealthy and raw
in front of guests, nuzzling
head up skirts
while I direct my mandarin mood.

Last week driving the baby sitter home.
She, unaware dog sat in the dark back seat,
talked on about the kids' behaviour.
On Huron Street the dog leaned forward
and licked her ear.
The car going 40 miles an hour
she seemed more amazed
at my driving ability
than my indiscretion.

It was only the dog I said.
Oh she said.
Me interpreting her reply all the way home.

Dates

It becomes apparent that I miss great occasions.
My birth was heralded by nothing
but the anniversary of Winston Churchill's marriage.
No monuments bled, no instruments
agreed on a specific weather.
It was a seasonal insignificance.

I console myself with my mother's eighth month.
While she sweated out her pregnancy in Ceylon
a servant ambling over the lawn
with a tray of iced drinks,
a few friends visiting her
to placate her shape, and I
drinking the life lines,
Wallace Stevens sat down in Connecticut
a glass of orange juice at his table
so hot he wore only shorts
and on the back of a letter
began to write 'The Well Dressed Man with a Beard'.

That night while my mother slept
her significant belly cooled
by the bedroom fan
Stevens put words together
that grew to sentences
and shaved them clean and
shaped them, the page suddenly
becoming thought where nothing had been,
his head making his hand
move where he wanted
and he saw his hand was saying
the mind is never finished, no, never
and I in my mother's stomach was growing
as were the flowers outside the Connecticut windows.

White Room

dear thin lady
you bend over your stomach
and your body is cool fruit

skin covers stray bones on your back
as sand envelops scattered fragments
of a wrecked aircraft

You are bending over your stomach
I am descending
like helicopters onto the plain

and we collapse
as flesh
within the angles of the room

Griffin of the night

I'm holding my son in my arms
sweating after nightmares
small me
fingers in his mouth
his other fist clenched in my hair
small me
sweating after nightmares

Letters & Other Worlds

'for there was no more darkness for him and, no doubt
like Adam before the fall, he could see in the dark'

My father's body was a globe of fear
His body was a town we never knew
He hid that he had been where we were going
His letters were a room he seldom lived in
In them the logic of his love could grow

My father's body was a town of fear
He was the only witness to its fear dance
He hid where he had been that we might lose him
His letters were a room his body scared

He came to death with his mind drowning.
On the last day he enclosed himself
in a room with two bottles of gin, later
fell the length of his body
so that brain blood moved
to new compartments
that never knew the wash of fluid
and he died in minutes of a new equilibrium.

His early life was a terrifying comedy
and my mother divorced him again and again.
He would rush into tunnels magnetized
by the white eye of trains
and once, gaining instant fame,
managed to stop a Perahara in Ceylon
— the whole procession of elephants dancers
local dignitaries — by falling
dead drunk onto the street.

As a semi-official, and semi-white at that,
the act was seen as a crucial
turning point in the Home Rule Movement
and led to Ceylon's independence in 1948.

(My mother had done her share too—
  her driving so bad
  she was stoned by villagers
  whenever her car was recognized)

For 14 years of marriage
each of them claimed he or she
was the injured party.
Once on the Colombo docks
saying goodbye to a recently married couple
my father, jealous
at my mother's articulate emotion,
dove into the waters of the harbour
and swam after the ship waving farewell.
My mother pretending no affiliation
mingled with the crowd back to the hotel.

Once again he made the papers
though this time my mother
with a note to the editor
corrected the report—saying he was drunk
rather than broken hearted at the parting of friends.
The married couple received both editions
of *The Ceylon Times* when their ship reached Aden.

And then in his last years
he was the silent drinker,

the man who once a week
disappeared into his room with bottles
and stayed there until he was drunk
and until he was sober.

There speeches, head dreams, apologies,
the gentle letters, were composed.
With the clarity of architects
he would write of the row of blue flowers
his new wife had planted,
the plans for electricity in the house,
how my half-sister fell near a snake
and it had awakened and not touched her.
Letters in a clear hand of the most complete empathy
his heart widening and widening and widening
to all manner of change in his children and friends
while he himself edged
into the terrible acute hatred
of his own privacy
till he balanced and fell
the length of his body
the blood screaming in
the empty reservoir of bones
the blood searching in his head without metaphor

Live Bait

While the ground was yet hot and smouldered, Yaada and some others returned.

They found the skull, fallen to the ground and caught in the black twisted roots of a tree. The stone was still between its jaws. Yaada took a stick and pointed.

'See!' she said, 'he was a great liar, and the word has choked him!'

Howard O'Hagan, *Tay John*

Rat Jelly

See the rat in the jelly
steaming dirty hair
frozen, bring it out on a glass tray
split the pie four ways and eat
I took great care cooking this treat for you
and tho it looks good to yuh
and tho it smells of the Westinghouse still
and tastes of exotic fish or
maybe the expensive arse of a cow
I want you to know it's rat
steamy dirty hair and still alive

(caught him last sunday
thinking of the fridge, thinking of you.

Breaking Green

Yesterday a Euclid took trees. Bright green
it beat against one till roots tilted
once more, machine in reverse, back ten yards
then forward and tore it off.
The Euclid moved away with it
returned, lifted ground
and levelled the remaining hollow.

And so earth was fresh, dark
a thick smell rising
where the snake lay.
The head grazed ribbon rich
eyes bright as gas.

The Euclid throttled and moved over the snake.
We watched blades dig in skin
and laughed, nothing had happened,
it continued to move bright at our boots.

The machine turned, tilted blade
used it as a spade
jerking onto the snake's back.
It slid away.
                    The driver angry then
jumped from the seat and caught the slither
head hooking round to snap his hand
but the snake was being swung already.

It was flying head out fast
as propellers forming green daze
a green gauze through which we saw the man
smile a grimace of pain as his arm tired
snake hurling round and round mouth arched **open**
till he turned and intercepted
the head with the Euclid blade.

Then he held the neck in his fist
brought his face close
to look at the crashed head
the staring eyes the same
all but the lower teeth
now locked in the skull.

The head was narrower now.
He blocked our looks at it.
The death was his. He
folded the scarless body
and tossed it like a river into the grass.

33

Philoctetes on the island

Sun moves broken in the trees
drops like a paw
turns sea to red leopard

I trap sharks and drown them
stuffing gills with sand
cut them with coral till
the blurred grey runs
red designs

And kill to fool myself alive
to leave all pity on the staggering body
in order not to shoot an arrow up
and let it hurl
down through my petalling skull
or neck vein, and lie
heaving round the wood in my lung.
That the end of thinking.
Shoot either eye of bird instead
and run and catch it in your hand.

One day a bird went mad
flew blind along the beach
smashed into a dropping wave
out again and plummeted.
Later knocked along the shore.

To slow an animal
you break its foot with a stone
so two run wounded
reel in the bush, flap
bodies at each other
till free of forest
it gallops broken in the sand,
then use a bow
and pin the tongue back down its throat.

With wind the rain wheels like a circus hoof,
aims at my eyes, rakes out the smell of animals
of stone moss, cleans me.
Branches fall like nightmares in the dark
till sun breaks up
and spreads wound fire at my feet

then they smell me,
the beautiful animals

Flirt and Wallace

The dog almost
tore my son's left eye out
with love, left a welt of passion
across his cheek

The other dog licks
the armpits of my shirt
for the salt
the smell and taste
that identifies me from others

With teeth which carry broken birds
with wet fur jaws that eat snow
suck the juice from branches
swallowing them all down
leaving their mouths tasteless, extroverted,
they graze our bodies with their love

Stuart's bird

We'd been talking about herons.

The next day Stuart
walking in his garden
trod on a bird,

it thrashed at his ankles
climbed into the air
4 feet above him
and flung a ribbon, a parabola of shit
over the creek and Stuart

Leo

Leo giggles coughing at his joke
sprawled on the bed, heels on the metal rail.
He holds his stomach like a fragile globe
cigarette smoke curls around his eyes.
See these hands? The blue red puckers
streak across his wrists like melted bangles.
I watch Leo in his white nightgown.
We shave on Thursdays see. . .

They shave on Thursdays while we watch
their moves to break the lock on razors.
Sport, gestures of being dangerous.
Leo dropped his on enamel
and it opened like a dream.
Others turned, circled him with praise,
the game a step further. And then.
What you going to do Leo
Go on Leo   Cut a screw up
And Leo standing there giggles
knowing, shaving soap scattered on his face,
he has to do something for them.

The Ceremony: A Dragon, a Hero,
and a Lady, by Uccello

The clouds burn blue, hang like sweat.
The green fields bounce the horse's paws.
A boy-knight shafts the dragon's eye
— the animal with a spine of claws.

In the foreground linked to dragon
with a leash of golden chain
dressed in silk there leans a lady
calmly holding to his pain.

From the mood I think it's Sunday
the monster's eye and throat blood strangled.
The horse's legs are bent like lightning.
The boy is perfect in his angle.

To Monsieur le Maire

I have the honour of sending you these few lines
as one of your countrymen
who has become a self taught artist
and is desirous that his native city
possess one of his works,
proposing that you purchase from me
a genre painting called
La Bohemienne Endormie
which measures 2.6 meters in width
and 1.9 in height.

>A wandering Negress
>playing her mandolin
>with her jar beside her
>(a vase containing water)
>sleeps deeply
>worn out by fatigue

>A lion wanders by
>detects her
>and doesn't devour her

>There's an effect of moonlight,
>very poetic.
>The scene takes place
>in a completely arid desert.
>The gypsy is dressed
>in oriental fashion

I will let it go for 2,000
or 1,800 francs
because I would be happy
to let the city of Laval
possess a remembrance
of one of its children.

In the hope that my offer
will be treated with favour,
accept, Monsieur le Maire,
the assurance
of my distinguished consideration.

Henri Rousseau
Artiste-Peintre
July 10, 1898

A bad taste

for Bob Fones

Moving to the forefronts of honesty
he comes to them with rat blood in his mouth.
He would turn them into ladies
place his brain at their hip.
Love his friends so completely
they would admit no artist in him to be found,
save eating an ice cream cone while reading Ezra Pound.
This friendship fat as God.

Meanwhile

*A PhD lecture by Mr S.H.Kung will take place today,
Thursday March 21 at 4 pm in Room 147, Medical
Science Building. Mr Kung will speak on 'Changes in
Dorsal Root Ganglia of the Rat following Peripheral
Nerve Section.'* U.W.O. News, Vol 13, no 31

Living in London he came closer to the rats.
There was rat chambers, rat curnoe,
the cunning rat urquhart, rat reaney and rat fones.
They travel so sly
you do not see the teeth
till in the operating room.

London Woman Fights Off Rat
*City police searched the Saunby Street area Thursday
night but found no trace of a small animal, described
as a rat, that tore a woman's umbrella to shreds while
she fought it off as she walked along the street.
Mrs Goldie King of 4 Saunby Street told police that
she was going to work when an animal she thought
was a rat lunged at her. Mrs King began hitting it with
her umbrella. The animal was scared off but not before the umbrella was ruined. Officials of the Humane
Society were notified.* London Free Press

The police are unaware of metaphormorphosis

Like snails the grey flecked university rats
leave their white refuse
across the corridors of the Paradise Lost Motel.
They identify with faculty
who have shifted into a state of melancholia
who arrive early with *The Globe and Mail*
and lock themselves in the washroom.
'How do you feel today then?'
'Lousy. . .'
They give inaccurate motives for that privacy. Still
the man combing the *Globe* for crazy meanings
won't have *his* picture in *artscanada*

In Toronto rats are cleaner, clipped.
They hold rat parties with cocktails on the terrace,
the rat in rational being scented with pronunciation.

But it was the rat in Ezra who wrote best,
that dirt thought we want as guest
travelling mad within the poem
eating up punctuation, who farts
heat into the line. You see
them shaved in the anthology.
You will be frozen and glib when
they aim for the sponge under the rib.

God being made fat
by eating the rat in us.

King Kong

In the yellow dust
of the light of the National Guard
he perishes magnanimous
tearing the world apart.
He pitches his balls accidentally
through a 14th storey window
gets a blow job
from the vacuum left by jets.

Up there our lady in his fingers
like a ring, so delicate
he must swallow what he loves
caressing with wounds
the ones who reach for him.

Then through the suburbs.
Impregnated the kitchen staff
of the Trade Winds Motel,
devoured half a Loblaws supermarket,
threw a Vic Tanney gymnasium around.
Last seen in Chicago with helicopters
cutting into his head like thorns.

So we renew him
capable in the zoo of night.

Sullivan and the iguana

The iguana is a comedian
erasing his body to death,
he is a gladiator retired after performance,
a general waiting for war overseas,
he is as secure about his sex as Tiresias

, thought Sullivan, his feet on the table.
In the room he looks across
to his green friend sleeping over the bulb
who has ignored the clover and vetch
that Sullivan picked in deserted lots.

Sullivan is alone
coiling in the room's light.
From his window he looks down
onto the traffic, people's heads,
he leaves his garbage and soiled grit outside the door.
The room has little furniture.
He pours meals out of tins and packages
and after midnight aims his body to the bed.
From there, every few weeks,
Sullivan watches the ancient friend undress
out of his skin in the rectangle of light
and become young and brilliant green.
Sullivan's brain exercises under the flesh.

Sullivan
, thought the iguana,
can turn the light on can turn it off
can open the cage
can hand in clover or hand in lettuce
can forget to change the water.

Loop

My last dog poem.
I leave behind all social animals
including my dog who takes
30 seconds dismounting from a chair.
Turn to the one
who appears again on roads
one eye torn out and chasing.

He is only a space filled
and blurred with passing,
transient as shit — will fade
to reappear somewhere else.

He survives the porcupine, cars, poison,
fences with their spasms of electricity.
Vomits up bones, bathes at night
in Holiday Inn swimming pools.

And magic in his act of loss.
The missing eye travels up
in a bird's mouth, and into the sky.
Departing family. It is loss only of flesh
no more than his hot spurt across a tree.

He is the one you see at Drive-Ins
tearing silent into garbage
while societies unfold in his sky.
The bird lopes into the rectangle nest of images

and parts of him move on.

Beaver

*'the Great Spirit was angry with the Beaver, and ordered
Weesaukejauk (The Flatterer) to drive them all from
the dry land into the water; and they became and continued very numerous; but the Great Spirit has been and
now is very angry with them and they are now all to
be destroyed'*

Beaver Beaver   slick wet hair
diver to the roots of air

                    You appear
eyes washed out, camouflaged.
I've seen your remnants of noise, the
sound of one hand clapping
when I turn and witness blank lake.
You have left — invisible as bullets
you take your dark traffic away from the sun.
If I was beginning again I'd want to be
Beaver, in this wet territory

Plucking his way through slime to nuzzle branch
he shapes forests in the image of his small star brain
(only low flying craft and beasts have seen the chaos plan)
only drunk architects have imagined the bloated structures
the lush corruption of his victims

Industry proposing sloth
maggot introversion
so all will go dark
deep dark black deep till
all his lands and seas shall sing
the humming quiet of the carbon

White Dwarfs

So saying, the merchant rose, and making his adieux, left the table with the air of one mortified at having been tempted by his own honest goodness, accidentally stimulated into making mad disclosures — to himself as to another — of the queer, unaccountable caprices of his natural heart.

Herman Melville, *The Confidence-Man*

We're at the graveyard

Stuart Sally Kim and I
watching still stars
or now and then sliding stars
like hawk spit to the trees.
Up there the clear charts,
the systems' intricate branches
which change with hours and solstices,
the bone geometry of moving from there, to there.

And down here—friends
whose minds and bodies
shift like acrobats to each other.
When we leave, they move
to an altitude of silence.

So our minds shape
and lock the transient,
parallel these bats
who organize the air
with thick blinks of travel.
Sally is like grey snow in the grass.
Sally of the beautiful bones
pregnant below stars.

Heron Rex

Mad kings
blood lines introverted, strained pure
so the brain runs in the wrong direction

they are proud of their heritage of suicides
— not the ones who went mad
balancing on that goddamn leg, but those

whose eyes turned off
the sun and imagined it
those who looked north, those who
forced their feathers to grow in
those who couldn't find the muscles in their arms
who drilled their beaks into the skin
those who could speak
and lost themselves in the foul connections
who crashed against black bars in a dream of escape
those who moved round the dials of imaginary clocks
those who fell asleep and never woke
who never slept and so dropped dead
those who attacked the casual eyes of children and were led away
and those who faced corners forever
those who exposed themselves and were led away
those who pretended broken limbs, epilepsy,
who managed to electrocute themselves on wire
those who felt their skin was on fire and screamed
                                    and were led away

There are ways of going
physically mad, physically
mad when you perfect the mind
where you sacrifice yourself for the race
when you are the representative when you allow
yourself to be paraded in the cages
celebrity a razor in the body

These small birds so precise
frail as morning neon
they are royalty melted down
they are the glass core at the heart of kings
yet 15 year old boys could enter the cage
and break them in minutes
as easily as a long fingernail

Near Elginburg

3 a.m. on the floor mattress.
In my pyjamas a moth beats frantic
my heart is breaking loose.

I have been dreaming of a man
who places honey on his forehead before sleep
so insects come tempted by liquid
to sip past it into the brain.
In the morning his head contains wings
and the soft skeletons of wasp.

Our suicide into nature.
That man's seduction
so he can beat the itch
against the floor and give in
move among the sad remnants
of those we have destroyed,
the torn code these animals ride to death on.
Grey fly on windowsill
white fish by the dock
heaved like a slimy bottle into the deep,
to end up as snake
heckled by children and cameras
as he crosses lawns of civilisation.

We lie on the floor mattress
lost moths walk on us
waterhole of flesh, want
this humiliation under the moon.
Till in the morning we are surrounded
by dark virtuous ships
sent by the kingdom of the loon.

Taking

It is the formal need
to suck blossoms out of the flesh
in those we admire
planting them private in the brain
and cause fruit in lonely gardens.

To learn to pour the exact arc
of steel still soft and crazy
before it hits the page.
I have stroked the mood and tone
of hundred year dead men and women
Emily Dickinson's large dog, Conrad's beard
and, for myself,
removed them from historical traffic.
Having tasted their brain. Or heard
the wet sound of a death cough.
Their idea of the immaculate moment is now.

The rumours pass on
the rumours pass on
are planted
till they become a spine.

Burning Hills

for Kris and Fred

So he came to write again
in the burnt hill region
north of Kingston. A cabin
with mildew spreading down walls.
Bullfrogs on either side of him.

Hanging his lantern of Shell Vapona Strip
on a hook in the centre of the room
he waited a long time. Opened
the Hilroy writing pad, yellow Bic pen.
Every summer he believed would be his last.
This schizophrenic season change, June to September,
when he deviously thought out plots
across the character of his friends.
Sometimes barren as fear going nowhere
or in habit meaningless as tapwater.
One year maybe he would come and sit
for 4 months and not write a word down
would sit and investigate colours, the
insects in the room with him.
What he brought: a typewriter
tins of ginger ale, cigarettes. A copy of *StrangeLove*,
of *The Intervals,* a postcard of Rousseau's *The Dream.*
His friends' words were strict as lightning
unclothing the bark of a tree, a shaved hook.
The postcard was a test pattern by the window
through which he saw growing scenery.
Also a map of a city in 1900.

Eventually the room was a time machine for him.
He closed the rotting door, sat down
thought of pieces of history. The first girl
who in a park near his school
put a warm hand into his trousers
unbuttoning and finally catching the spill
across her wrist, he in the maze of her skirt.
She later played the piano
when he had tea with the parents.
He remembered that surprised—
he had forgotten for so long.
Under raincoats in the park on hot days.

The summers were layers of civilisation in his memory
they were old photographs he didn't look at anymore
for girls in them were chubby not as perfect as in his mind
and his ungovernable hair was shaved to the edge of skin.
His friends leaned on bicycles
were 16 and tried to look 21
the cigarettes too big for their faces.
He could read those characters easily
undisguised as wedding pictures.
He could hardly remember their names
though they had talked all day, exchanged styles
and like dogs on a lawn hung around the houses of girls
waiting for night and the devious sex-games with their simple plots.
Sex a game of targets, of throwing firecrackers
at a couple in a field locked in hand-made orgasms,

singing dramatically in someone's ear along with the record
'How do you think I feel / You know our love's not real
The one you're mad about / Is just a gad-about
How do you think I feel'
He saw all that complex tension the way his children would.

There is one picture that fuses the 5 summers.
Eight of them are leaning against a wall
arms around each other
looking into the camera and the sun
trying to smile at the unseen adult photographer
trying against the glare to look 21 and confident.
The summer and friendship will last forever.
Except one who was eating an apple. That was him
oblivious to the significance of the moment.
Now he hungers to have that arm around the next shoulder.
The wretched apple is fresh and white.

Since he began burning hills
the Shell strip has taken effect.
A wasp is crawling on the floor
tumbling over, its motor fanatic.
He has smoked 5 cigarettes.
He has written slowly and carefully
with great love and great coldness.
When he finishes he will go back
hunting for the lies that are obvious.

Looking into THE PROJECTOR

The horse is falling off the skyscraper
staggering through the air.
He will never reach
pavements of men and cars,
he is caught between
the 70th and 72nd floor of someone's brain.
The side of the building is a highway
he has left, bobbing dobbin.
A few frames later he will burst
through the window-washers' platform
and *they* will fall but he continues
to pulse, held by the nightmare's chain.
(The value of rhyme and pun being they tell
of the polarities of the tale)
Dobbin and Bobbin.

For someone has left the saddle dying.
The air has got into his body
it is ripping him apart he has been
thrown like a suitcase out
of the window by God.
The air is moving the wrong way in him
he will be consumed before ever reaching the ground.

Fabulous shadow

They fished me from this Quebec river
the face blurred glass, bones of wing
draping my body like nets
in a patterned butterfly

and peeled green weed from scorched shoulders
and the dried wax from my thighs

King Kong meets Wallace Stevens

Take two photographs—
Wallace Stevens and King Kong
(Is it significant that I eat bananas as I write this?)

Stevens is portly, benign, a white brush cut
striped tie. Businessman but
for the dark thick hands, the naked brain
the thought in him.

Kong is staggering
lost in New York streets again
a spawn of annoyed cars at his toes.
The mind is nowhere.
Fingers are plastic, electric under the skin.
He's at the call of Metro-Goldwyn-Mayer.

Meanwhile W. S. in his suit
is thinking chaos is thinking fences.
In his head the seeds of fresh pain
his exorcising,
the bellow of locked blood.

The hands drain from his jacket,
pose in the murderer's shadow.

'The gate in his head'

for Victor Coleman

Victor, the shy mind
revealing the faint scars
coloured strata of the brain,
not clarity but the sense of shift

a few lines, the tracks of thought

Landscape of busted trees
the melted tires in the sun
Stan's fishbowl
with a book inside
turning its pages
like some sea animal
camouflaging itself
the typeface clarity
going slow blonde in the sun full water

My mind is pouring chaos
in nets onto the page.
A blind lover, dont know
what I love till I write it out.
And then from Gibson's your letter
with a blurred photograph of a gull.
Caught vision. The stunning white bird
an unclear stir.

And that is all this writing should be then.
The beautiful formed things caught at the wrong moment
so they are shapeless, awkward
moving to the clear.

Spider Blues

'Well I made them laugh, I wish I could make them cry.'

David McFadden

My wife has a smell that spiders go for.
At night they descend saliva roads
down to her dreaming body.
They are magnetized by her breath's rhythm,
leave their own constructions
for succulent travel across her face and shoulder.
My own devious nightmares
are struck to death by her shrieks.

About the spiders.
Having once tried to play piano
and unable to keep both hands
segregated in their intent
I admire the spider, his control classic,
his eight legs finicky,
making lines out of the juice in his abdomen.
A kind of writer I suppose.
He thinks a path and travels
the emptiness that was there
leaves his bridge behind
looking back saying Jeez
did I do that?
and uses his ending

to swivel to new regions
where the raw of feelings exist.

Spiders like poets are obsessed with power.
They write their murderous art which sleeps
like stars in the corner of rooms,
a mouth to catch audiences
weak   broken   sick

And spider comes to fly, says
Love me I can kill you, love me
my intelligence has run rings about you
love me, I kill you for the clarity that
comes when roads I make are being made
love me, antisocial, lovely.
And fly says, O no
no your analogies are slipping
no I choose who I die with
you spider poets are all the same
you in your close vanity of making,
you minor drag, your saliva stars always
soaking up the liquid from our atmosphere.
And the spider in his loathing
crucifies his victims in his spit
making them the art he cannot be.

So. The ending we must arrive at.
                              ok folks.
Nightmare for my wife and me:

It was a large white room
and the spiders had thrown
their scaffolds off the floor
onto four walls and the ceiling.
They had surpassed themselves this time
and with the white roads
their eight legs built with speed
they carried her up — her whole body
into the dreaming air so gently
she did not wake or scream.
What a scene. So many trails
the room was a shattered pane of glass.
Everybody clapped, all the flies.
They came and gasped, all
everybody cried at the beauty
ALL
except the working black architects
and the lady locked in their dream   their theme

The Vault

Having to put forward candidates for God
I nominate Henri Rousseau and Dr Bucke,
tired of the lizard paradise
whose image banks renew off the flesh of others
— those stories that hate, which are remnants and insults.
Refresh where plants breed to the edge of the dream.

I have woken to find myself covered in white sheets
walls and doors, food.
There was no food in the world I left
where you ate the rich air. The bodies of small birds
who died while flying fell into your mouth.
Fruit dripped through your thirst to the earth.

All night the traffic of apes floats across the sky
a worm walks through the gaze of a lion
some birds live all their evenings on one branch.

They are held by the celebration of God's wife.
In Rousseau's *The Dream* she is the naked lady
who has been animal and tree
her breast a suckled orange.
The fibres and fluids of their moral nature
have seeped within her frame.

The hand is outstretched
her fingers move out in
mutual transfusion to the place.
Our low speaking last night
was barely audible among the grunt
of mongrel meditation.

She looks to the left
for that is the direction we leave in
when we fall from her room of flowers.

Charles Darwin pays a visit, December 1971

View of the coast of Brazil.
A man stood up to shout
at the image of a sailing ship
which was a vast white bird from over the sea
and now ripping its claws into the ocean.
Faded hills of March
painted during the cold morning.
On board ship Charles Darwin sketched clouds.

One of these days the Prime Mover will
paint the Prime Mover out of his sky.
I want a ... centuries being displaced
... faith.

> '23rd of June, 1832.
> He caught sixty-eight species
> of a particularly minute beetle.'

The blue thick leaves who greeted him
animals unconscious of celebration
moved slowly into law.
Adam with a watch.
Look past and future, (I want a...),
ease our way out of the structures
this smell of the cogs
and diamonds we live in.

I am waiting for a new ship, so new
we will think the lush machine
an animal of God.
Weary from travelling over the air and the water
it will sink to its feet at our door.

Birth of Sound

At night the most private of a dog's long body groan.
It comes with his last stretch
in the dark corridor outside our room.
The children turn.
A window tries to split with cold
the other dog hoofing the carpet for lice.
We're all alone.

White Dwarfs

This is for people who disappear
for those who descend into the code
and make their room a fridge for Superman
—who exhaust costume and bones that could perform flight,
who shave their moral so raw
they can tear themselves through the eye of a needle
this is for those people
that hover and hover
and die in the ether peripheries

There is my fear
of no words   of
falling without words
over and over   of
mouthing the silence
Why do I love most
among my heroes those
who sail to that perfect edge
where there is no social fuel
Release of sandbags
to understand their altitude —

          that silence of the third cross
          3rd man hung so high and lonely
          we dont hear him say
          say his pain, say his unbrotherhood
          What has he to do with the smell of ladies
          can they eat off his skeleton of pain?

The Gurkhas in Malaya
cut the tongues of mules
so they were silent beasts of burden
in enemy territories
after such cruelty what could they speak of anyway
And Dashiell Hammett in success
suffered conversation and moved
to the perfect white between the words

This white that can grow
is fridge, bed,
is an egg — most beautiful
when unbroken, where
what we cannot see is growing
in all the colours we cannot see

there are those burned out stars
who implode into silence
after parading in the sky
after such choreography what would they wish to speak of   anyway

Some of these poems first appeared in the following magazines: Canadian Forum, Fiddlehead, Quarry, Alphabet, Duel, Writing, artscanada, Open Letter, IS, Unicorn portfolio, Ant's Forefoot, White Pelican, Tuatara, Blew Ointment, Talon. And in the following anthologies: *Made in Canada* (Oberon), and *Fifteen Canadian Poets* (Oxford). 'To Monsieur le Maire' is an extract from the book *The Banquet Years* by Roger Shattuck.

Most of them were written in London, Ontario or in the country east or north of Kingston — around Inverary, Elginburg, Battersea and Gananoque. Some in Toronto. They consist of shorter poems written between 1966, when *The Dainty Monsters* was finished, and the summer of 1972. They were written before during and after two longer works — *The Man with Seven Toes* and *The Collected Works of Billy the Kid* — when the right hand thought it knew what the left hand was doing.

Designed and printed at The Coach House Press.

ISBN 0 88910 107 8 softcover
ISBN 0 88910 107 6 hardcover

Front Cover: A detail from an old stained glass window which originally decorated a nursery school in London, Ontario. Thanks to Anne Garwood who now has it, and thanks to the unknown artist.
Back cover photo by Kim Ondaatje.